W9-CML-291

Copyright © 1993 by Catherine and Laurence Anholt

All rights reserved.

First U.S. edition 1993
Published in Great Britain in 1993
by Walker Books Ltd., London.

Library of Congress Cataloging-in-Publication Data

Anholt, Catherine.
Toddlers / Catherine and Laurence Anholt.—1st U.S. ed.
(A Candlewick toddler book)
Summary: Follows, in rhyming text and illustrations, the many
activities and moods of a variety of busy toddlers.
ISBN 1-56402-242-0
[1. Stories in rhyme.]   I. Anholt, Laurence.   II. Title.   III. Series.
PZ8.3.A245To   1993
[E]—dc20   92-54588

10 9 8 7 6 5 4 3 2 1

Printed in Hong Kong

The pictures in this book were
done in pen and watercolor.

Candlewick Press
2067 Massachusetts Avenue
Cambridge, Massachusetts 02140

Toddlers

Catherine and Laurence Anholt

CANDLEWICK PRESS
CAMBRIDGE, MASSACHUSETTS

We are the toddlers . . .

teeter,

totter,

topsy,

turvy,

toddlers are all round and curvy.

Toddlers come in different sizes .

I am big,

we are small,

I am hardly here at all.

They are all different . . .

I am sleepy,

I am grumpy,

I am noisy,

I am jumpy,

I am sad,

I am sweet,

I can stand on my two feet.

Toddlers love to play . . .

up and down,

roundabout,

upside down,

in and out.

Toddlers can . . .

hop like a rabbit,

bark like a dog,

climb like a bear,

jump like a frog.

Toddlers make lots of noise . . .

dancing,

singing,

banging,

ringing.

Toddlers like eating . . .

I like jam,

we like bread,

I like Jell-O on my head.

Toddlers are always busy . . .

crawling,

sitting,

peeping,

running,

sleeping.